Once Upon a Reptar

By Kitty Richards

Illustrated by Barry Goldberg

SCHOLASTIC INC.

New York Toronto London Auckland Sydney
Mexico City New Delhi Hong Kong

Based on the TV series *Rugrats*® created by Klasky/Csupo Inc. and Paul Germain as seen on Nickelodeon®

No part of this publication may be reproduced in whole or in part, or stored in a retrieval system, or transmitted in any form or by any means, electronic, mechanical, photocopying, recording, or otherwise, without written permission of the publisher. For information regarding permission, write to Simon Spotlight, an imprint of Simon & Schuster Children's Publishing Division, 1230 Avenue of the Americas, New York, NY 10020.

ISBN 0-439-06756-1

12 11 10 9 8 7 6 5 4 3 2 1   9/9 0 1 2 3 4/0

Manufactured in China   40

First Scholastic printing, April 1999

"So how about a bedtime story, sprout?" Grandpa Lou asked Tommy.

"Let's see, we've read 'Hansel and Gretel,' 'Goldilocks and the Three Bears,' and 'Jack in the Beanstalk.' Tonight I think we'll read my favorite fairy tale, 'Little Red Riding Hood.'"

He began to read all about Little Red Riding Hood and what happened when she met the Big Bad Wolf. "And they all lived happily ever after," he finished. "Except for the wolf, of course."

Then Grandpa picked Tommy up and tucked him into his crib. "Good night, scout. Don't let the bedbugs bite."

The next night Tommy slept over at Chuckie's house. "Hey, Chuckie, how 'bout a bedtime story?" asked Tommy. "I know lotsa good hairy tales."

Chuckie pulled the blanket up to his chin. "I dunno, Tommy," he said. "Are they scary?"

"No, they're not scary at all," Tommy said. "Hairy tales are fun!"

And he began . . .

Once a pony time there was a dinosaur named Little Reptar Riding
Hood. One day his mom asked him to take a baskey full of Reptar
cereal over to his grandma, who lived on the other side of the forest.
On the way there, he saw a trail of bread crumbs, and he followed it
and followed it until he came to . . .

a gingerbread house! It was covered with lots of yummy candy. Reptar was really hungry, so he breaked off a piece of the gingerbread roof and one of the candy canes and gobbled them up. Then he went inside and found . . .

three bowls of Reptar cereal on the table! One was too big, one was too small, and one was just right. So Reptar ate them all.

Then he got sleepy and went upstairs and found three beds. One was too hard, one was too soft, and one was just right. . . .

But someone was sleeping in it! It was Grandma Reptar!

Reptar said, "Grandma, what red eyes you have!"

And his grandma said, "the better to see you with, my dear."

Reptar said, "Grandma, what small ears you have!"

And Grandma said, "What?"

Reptar said, "Grandma, what big teeth you have!"

And Grandma said, "the better to eat Reptar cereal with! Did you bring me some?"

Suddenly Reptar turned
around and ran out of the house.
He wanted all the Reptar cereal for
himself! He ran and ran until he came
to a magic beanstalk.

Then he climbed up so Grandma Reptar wouldn't find him.

But his grandma chopped down the beanstalk!

And then she and Reptar sat down for breakfast.

"And they all lived happily never after," Tommy said.
Chuckie smiled. "That was the best hairy tale I ever heard."